Look for more

titles:

TWO of a kind™ Diaries

Shore Thing

by Judy Katschke
from the series created by
Robert Griffard & Howard Adler

HarperEntertainment
An Imprint of HarperCollinsPublishers
A PARACHUTE PRESS BOOK

A PARACHUTE PRESS BOOK

Parachute Publishing, L.L.C.
156 Fifth Avenue
Suite 302
New York, NY 10010

Published by
HarperEntertainment
An Imprint of HarperCollins*Publishers*
10 East 53rd Street, New York, NY 10022-5299

TWO OF A KIND books created and produced by
Parachute Press, L.L.C., in cooperation with Dualstar Publications,
a division of Dualstar Entertainment Group, Inc.,
published by HarperEntertainment, an imprint of
HarperCollins Publishers.

For information address HarperCollins Publishers Inc.,
10 East 53rd Street, New York, NY 10022-5299.

ISBN 0-06-106657-5

First printing: June 2001

Printed in the United States of America

Visit HarperEntertainment on the World Wide Web at
www.harpercollins.com

10 9 8 7 6 5 4 3 2 1

Chapter 1

Saturday

Dear Diary,

Sorry if my handwriting is a little jerky, but I'm sitting on this bus rolling down something called the 100-Mile Highway in Florida. And the last time I checked we still had about fifty five miles to go.

See, my twin sister Ashley and I are on this really cool school trip. I know, I know—it's the first week of summer vacation. But when I tell you all about this trip you'll see why Ashley and I decided to stick around. Oh, and since you're a brand-new diary (my old one filled up pretty fast), I'll clue you in on all the details.

Ashley and I are First Formers at a boarding school called The White Oak Academy for Girls in New Hampshire. First Form is the school's way of saying seventh grade. That took some getting used to. So did eating oatmeal every morning for breakfast, another White Oak tradition. Just like these summer vacation school trips.

There's a camping trip to Maine, a sightseeing trip to New York City, and a trip to a tiny island off the coast of Florida in an area called the Keys.

Ashley and I chose to spend two weeks on the island at Camp Coral Reef. Then we'll be going to Miami for a week on the beach.

I know what you're thinking, Diary. That Ashley and I are off to roast hot dogs and paint ceramic frogs in arts and crafts. NOT! In this camp we'll learn all about marine biology—fancy words for fish and underwater plants. We're also going to try our hands at wildlife photography, deep sea fishing, and scuba diving.

Diary, when I heard about the scuba diving I was so there. But Ashley needed a little convincing. . . .

"You mean I'll have to wear a mask and flippers, and an oxygen tank?" Ashley asked me when I read the brochure out loud.

"Sure!" I said. "How else are you going to get up-close and personal with a barracuda?"

"I'm not sure I want to," Ashley said.

No kidding! Ashley and I may be twins but we're as different as two  snowflakes. I dig sports, drama, and watching the Cubs game in my sweats. Ashley likes ballet, boys, and clothes, clothes, clothes! Get the picture?

Shore Thing

I can't wait to scuba dive! Of course, we have to get our scuba certificates first, but no problem! I beat Ashley at holding our breaths in the bathtub when we were little.

Now here's the neatest part: Some of our best buds from school are going to Camp Coral Reef, too.

"What made you sign up, Cheryl?" I asked during breakfast on our last day of school.

"Are you kidding?" Cheryl Miller said. "After being in New England all winter, I want as much sun as I can get!"

"So do I!" Summer Sorenson said. "I want to kick up my tan before I go home to Malibu. It's definitely fading."

Everyone looked at Summer as if she were from outer space. Her tan will never fade. It's for life!

As for Elise Van Hook, she wants to study marine animals before visiting her Peace Corps volunteer parents in Fiji.

"So you can learn to recognize the natural wildlife?" Ashley asked Elise.

Elise nodded. "I definitely need to know what's poisonous and what's not!" she said.

And then there's Phoebe Cahill. Phoebe is Ashley's roommate and the editor of the First Form newspaper, the *White Oak Acorn*. She loves poetry, classic movies, and vintage clothes. But *not* sports. In fact, Phoebe's idea of the great outdoors is an open-air flea market.

"If you're not a sports nut, why are you going to Florida?" I asked Phoebe. "It's all about water sports!"

"I'm going to write about the trip for the fall issue of the *Acorn*," Phoebe said. "I don't intend to get anywhere near a scuba tank."

"Lucky you," I heard Ashley mutter.

And if you're wondering about boys—some First Formers from the Harrington School for Boys are going, too. Like our cousin Jeremy Burke, who's dying to learn scuba diving. I'm not surprised. He's been blowing bubbles in his milk since he was in kindergarten.

Other Harrington guys are Seth Samuels, Justin Martinez, and Ross Lambert. Ashley has had a crush on Ross since we started White Oak. And after kissing him in the school play, that crush became more of a—CRUNCH! Ashley and Ross had sort of a misunderstanding this spring. But now they're a couple again.

Shore Thing

Ashley is sitting next to me writing in her diary and eating the honey roasted nuts we got on the plane to Miami. She has this serious look on her face as if she's writing a term paper. What's her problem?

Anyway, Diary, gotta go. Jeremy just tossed a rubber cockroach on my lap. And it's time to get even!

Dear Diary,

What was I thinking? Okay, Florida is really great-looking, with all those swaying palm trees and bright blue skies. But once we hit Camp Coral Reef it's going to be downhill all the way. Why? I'll tell you. . . .

A few weeks ago Cheryl and I were in the school bookstore. Cheryl was looking for a travel book on Florida. I was just . . . looking.

But just as I was about to grab a book about ballet, I saw a big paperback called *The Worst That Can Happen.* I flipped through it and almost flipped myself.

The book tells you everything that can go wrong—anytime, anyplace. Like there's a gross chapter on the stuff you can find in your chicken nuggets. And what can happen to your toenails after you go for a pedicure. (You don't want to know.)

But there was one chapter that really made my teeth curl. A chapter on water sports!

"Cheryl, check it out!" I called. "Did you know that jellyfish are practically invisible? That's why people step on them and get stung!"

Cheryl looked at the book and laughed. "Come on, Ashley," she said. "You can't go through life expecting the worst all the time."

"Bad things do happen, you know," I said.

Cheryl shrugged. "Then if someone tosses you a lemon, you have to make the best of it— make lemonade!" she declared.

"Lemonade," I said, flipping through the book. "I'll bet there's a chapter on lemons, too. And what happens when you swallow too many seeds—"

"Girlfriend, put that nasty book down!" Cheryl ordered.

But I had other plans.

"I'm buying this book," I told Cheryl. "Maybe it's not too late to change Mary-Kate's mind about Camp Coral Reef."

"You're showing that book to your sister?" Cheryl asked. "Mary-Kate 'Fearless' Burke?"

"No way!" I said. "She'd just call me a wimp."

Instead I tried to talk Mary-Kate out of going to Florida and into going to New York City.

"New York?" Mary-Kate asked as we hung out in the student lounge. "Why New York?"

"Because I want to wake up in a city that never sleeps!" I exclaimed. "I want to see its treasures. The museums, the theaters—"

"The stores?" Mary-Kate joked.

"Hey," I said. "Can I help it if I'd rather try on clam diggers than dig for clams?"

It was no use. Mary-Kate was set on the Keys and I was set for *disaster!*

But later I found out that Ross Lambert was going to Camp Coral Reef, too. That's when I gave in. I mean, Ross and I probably won't see each other for the rest of the summer. And he's the only boy I've ever liked. Okay, okay, there've been more. Lots more. But not all of them liked me back!

In the end it was Dad in Chicago who made the decision. He thought the camp would be a "good educational experience." Spoken like a true college professor.

Whoops! Time out. One of the campers dropped an earring on the bus and everyone's looking for it. And guess what? It belongs to a boy!

I'm back. And my Coral Reef nightmare has already begun. Right now we're sitting outside the Main House while Mrs. Clare, our assistant headmistress, checks us in. Mrs. Clare is cool. She came on the trip with a supply of sun hats, sunscreen, and packets of oatmeal. I guess the White Oak tradition lives on, even in Florida.

When the bus pulled up to the camp a half hour ago we were all confused.

"This is a camp?" Jeremy asked. "Where are the bunks? And the mess hall? And the softball field?"

"This isn't that kind of camp, Jeremy," Mrs. Clare said. "We'll all be staying inside the beach house and studying at the Marine Center down the road."

Mrs. Clare pointed out of the bus window. "In fact," she said, "there's the pool where you'll be learning how to scuba dive."

I stared at the pool. It looked cool and crystal clear and safe. I felt better until all the kids started pumping their fists in the air and chanting, "Scuba! Scuba! Scuba!"

That's when I felt really sick.

I mean, haven't they ever seen *Jaws*?

Chapter 2

Sunday

Hi, Diary!

Here it is. My first full day at Camp Coral Reef and all I can say is—this place rocks!

We spent most of the day getting to know each other (even though we already do!) and meeting the camp staff.

The director of the camp is a guy named Sid Pepper. Sid has long gray hair that he ties back in a ponytail. He wears white shorts and T-shirts with corny sayings like "Florida—the Funshine State." He also plays the guitar and sings about ships and whales. That's cool, because the only whale song I know is "Baby Beluga."

There's a counselor for fishing and boating named Brad. A counselor for photography named Keith. And a scuba instructor named Jenny. They all seem nice and their tans make Summer look pale.

And you should check out the big house we're all staying in. It has this huge porch that wraps all the way around. And all of the rooms have wicker furniture and fans on the ceiling.

"It's like something out of a 1930s movie!" Phoebe gasped. Just so you know, Diary, Phoebe likes vintage movies as much as she likes vintage clothes.

And you should see the dining room. It's nothing like the one back at White Oak.

"Where are the gargoyles?" Elise joked when we walked in. "And the paintings of the ex-head-mistresses?"

Instead there are layers of fishnets on the ceiling and wooden fish on the walls. And inside a big wicker cage are real, live parrots!

"Polly want a cracker?" Summer asked a parrot.

"Polly doesn't want a cracker," Jeremy said. "He wants a cheeseburger and fries. Trust me."

What I like best about Florida are all the palm trees. My favorites are the tall, skinny ones. Ashley likes the ones that look like cheerleader pom-poms. But the best is the beach in back of our house. The sand is sugar-white and the Atlantic Ocean is the bluest blue I've ever seen. Is this paradise or what?

Too bad Ashley doesn't think so. After lugging our bags to our room I expected the usual argument— "who gets the bed by the window?" So was I amazed when Ashley wanted the bed against the wall.

"You never know what exotic creatures might crawl through the window, Mary-Kate," Ashley said. "I read all about mosquitoes that carry malaria!"

"Malaria?" I asked. "Where'd you learn that?"

"Nowhere," Ashley said quickly. I caught her stuffing something deep into her backpack.

I held out my hand. "Let me see it. If we're going to share a room there'll be no secrets."

Ashley's shoulders dropped. She slowly pulled out a book and held it up.

"The Worst That Can Happen?" I cried.

Ashley told me all about the book. That's when I laughed out loud.

"It's not funny," Ashley said. "There's even a whole chapter on water sports. Like, did you know diving too deep could make your lungs explode? And your eyeballs pop?"

"But you won the swim team medal three years ago," I told Ashley.

"Yeah," Ashley said. "But I wasn't being chased by a thirty-foot alligator!"

"Alligators stick to the swamps," I said. "Don't you remember that nature show on TV? Where that Australian guy actually

wrestled the alligator with his bare hands?"

"You saw it," Ashley said. "I had my eyes closed!"

"What a wuss!" I laughed. "Maybe you *should* have gone to New York. The only alligators there are in shoe stores."

Ashley's eyes grew as big as Frisbees.

"A wuss?" she gasped. "I am not a wuss!"

"Are too," I said. "And thanks to that book, I'll bet you won't even make it through the next few weeks of camp. You'll be too scared to do anything!"

Ashley's face turned red. She folded her arms across her chest. "Oh, yeah?" she said. "Well, I bet that I can get through camp with flying colors! Not only that, I'm even going to pass my scuba test—the first time!"

"Oh, yeah?" I said. "Well, so am I. The bet is on!"

We hooked pinkies, which is what we always do when we make a bet. Then I told Ashley that the loser had to clean the winner's side of her dorm room at school. For six whole months!

"Not fair!" Ashley shrieked. "My side of my dorm room only needs a broom. Your side of your room needs a—bulldozer!"

Blah, blah, blah. Let her complain. All I can say

is, it'll be nice having maid service for a while! And my roomie Campbell will love having a clean room for a change!

Oh, well. Gotta run. There's a moonlight party on the beach tonight. I guess that means I don't need sunscreen!

Dear Diary,

My *Worst That Can Happen* book left out an important chapter—going on vacation with your twin sister!

Now I have to prove to Mary-Kate that I can survive the next two weeks without a hitch. That means fishing, boating, and worst of all—scuba diving!

"What was I *thinking*?" I asked myself all day.

Luckily there was a beach party at night to take my mind off the bet. While everyone else joined the limbo contest, I shared a beach blanket with Ross. We stared out at the ocean and talked.

"After camp ends I won't see you for two whole months," Ross said. "What are we going to do?"

Two months? The thought of not seeing Ross made my heart drop. But then I had an idea . . .

"I know!" I said. "You have a cousin who lives in Chicago. Why don't you visit him over the summer?"

Ross's eyes lit up. He seemed to like the idea.

"I'll ask my mom and dad," he said. "If they say yes, then it's a go!"

I thought of something else.

"We can even go to the 4-You concert," I said. "They're playing in Chicago in August!"

In case I haven't told you, Diary, 4-You is our favorite singing group. They totally rule!

Ross smiled and gave me a high-five. I would have preferred a kiss but who's complaining?

Just then my cousin Jeremy walked over. His cheeks were puffed out like he was chewing on something.

"Do you like seafood?" Jeremy asked me through his full mouth.

"Seafood?" I said. "Sure."

Jeremy popped his mouth open to show me what was inside. "*See food!*" He laughed. "Get it?"

Ross laughed, but I was totally grossed. I grabbed a sponge football and tossed it at my cousin's head.

"Hey!" Jeremy complained.

"Nice pass!" a boy's voice said.

I spun around. Standing behind us was a boy of about thirteen. He had short brown hair and the lightest green eyes I ever saw.

"Ashley, this is Devon Benjamin," Ross said. "He's starting Harrington in September."

"Why weren't you on the plane or the bus with the rest of us?" I asked Devon.

"I hooked up with you guys today," Devon explained. "I live here in Florida. Over in Daytona Beach."

"You live by a beach?" I asked. "You must be a great swimmer."

"I—" Devon started to say.

"Devon practically has gills!" Jeremy interrupted. "He told me he's been scuba diving since he was ten!"

"Ten and a half," Devon said.

"Scuba?" I gulped. I was having such a good time, I had almost forgotten about it.

The boys went off to join the limbo contest. I sat on the beach towel alone. But not for long.

"What's wrong, Ashley?" Mary-Kate asked as she sat down beside me. "Is there a chapter in your book about limbo?"

"Nope," I said coolly. "I just don't feel like playing right now." *The Worst That Can Happen* said you could break your back doing the limbo, but I wasn't going to mention that part to Mary-Kate.

"I can't wait until tomorrow," Mary-Kate said. She rubbed her hands. "It's our first day of activities. And last I looked, deep-sea fishing was on the schedule."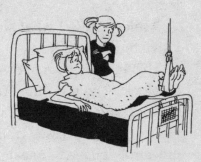

Deep-sea fishing? As in barracudas? Sharks? Seasickness? I tried not to let Mary-Kate see me shudder.

Instead I plastered on a big smile.

"Deep-sea fishing!" I cheered. "Bring it on!"

Just then I heard a loud yelp. I looked up and saw everyone running over to Seth Samuels.

"What happened?" I asked Cheryl.

"Seth just got stung by a big old jellyfish!" Cheryl said. "It was right under the limbo pole."

Diary, I've got to go. I have to finish reading up on jellyfish!

Chapter 3

Monday

Hey, Diary,

Ashley can say what she wants, but I love the Florida Keys.

This morning we had fresh fruit for breakfast. The last time I ate a papaya was back in Chicago and it was dried and rolled up. And I'll bet the ex-headmistresses from the 1800s never tasted pineapple-guava oatmeal.

But you have to be careful what you say around those parrots. I know because we picked the table right next to the parrot cage. Big mistake!

"You guys," Cheryl muttered over her pineapple juice. "Check out Mrs. Clare's sun hat!"

I glanced at the next table. Mrs. Clare's straw hat was the size of a manhole cover. It was so huge she had to tilt her head to get through the door.

"Too weird!" Elise snickered.

I heard a loud squawk. The red-and-green macaw named Taco began ruffling his feathers and rolling his head.

"Mrs. Clare!" he screeched. "Too weird! Arrk!"

Mrs. Clare glared at us from the next table.

"Thanks a lot, cracker breath!" Cheryl muttered to Taco.

Shore Thing

It was a good thing we had a big breakfast because this was our first day of activities.

First stop was the Marine Center. I expected some little fish museum, but was I wrong. The big glass building with the whale sculpture out front has classrooms and laboratories—even an aquarium filled with live sea creatures. Keith pointed out  fish I never heard of, like Harlequin Bass, Parrot Fish, and Nassau Groupers. There's a whole room filled with marine fossils and a six-foot giant squid hanging from the ceiling!

The squid may have been dead, but that didn't stop my sister from totally flipping out.

"Didn't you see?" Ashley cried to Keith. "He just waved at me! With his tentacles!"

"Don't tell me there's a chapter on the worst that can happen with a dead squid!" I joked.

"As a matter of fact there is," Ashley said. "A woman in Denver ate bad squid and was sick for weeks!"

Boy, Diary. Winning this bet is going to be even easier than I thought!

Dear Diary,

After we were totally freaked out by a giant dead squid, Brad took us fishing on the high seas. It wasn't very high, just enough to make most of us turn a pale shade of green from seasickness.

As Sid sailed the fishing boat out to sea, Brad made an announcement.

"Listen," he said. "We're not going to keep any of the fish we catch. We're going to throw them back into the sea. But first we're going to learn how to hook bait."

No problem, I thought. We'll probably use pieces of stale bread. Or those fuzzy little tackle things you see people fishing with.

Then all of a sudden Brad reached down and pulled out a small pail of worms! No, not the gummy type. These were the real things!

"We have sandworms and bloodworms," Brad told us. As if they were toppings in a frozen yogurt store.

"Or you can use these guys," Brad said. He reached into a tackle box and pulled out a jar of tiny dried-up fish. "They're not alive and it's a good thing because you have to hook them through their eyes."

My mouth dropped open. I mean, did you ever hear of anything so yucky?

Luckily I wasn't the only grossed-out camper. Justin said he had 'worm-phobia.' Summer turned pale for the first time this year. Phoebe almost dropped her reporter pad and pencil overboard.

"Okay," Brad said. He picked up a worm between two fingers. "Who wants to go first?"

"Why don't you go, Ashley?" Jeremy called out.

"Me?" I asked. "Why me?"

Jeremy faced the other campers. "Because when Ashley was in kindergarten she found a tiny worm in the sandbox," he said. "And she totally freaked out!"

"Oh, I remember!" Mary-Kate said. "Ashley climbed to the top of the monkey bars and wouldn't come down for an hour!"

My cheeks burned as everyone laughed.

Now the whole camp thought I was a baby.

"Oh, Brad!" I called, raising my hand. "I'll go first!"

"Are you sure, Ashley?" Brad asked. "If you don't like worms—"

"Are you kidding?" I scoffed. "I eat worms like that for breakfast. Bring 'em on!"

I threw back my shoulders and marched over to

Brad. I expected him to hand me a worm. Instead he pointed to the pail and said, "Dig in!"

"Dig in?" I gulped. "O-o-okay."

I tried to blur my eyes as I kneeled by the pail. Then I played a little mind game.

These are not worms, I told myself as I reached in. These are yummy licorice whips. Cherry licorice whips. . . .

It worked until I actually touched the worms. Cherry licorice whips didn't squirm or wiggle!

"Excuse me?" I gulped. I wiped my hand off on my shorts. "I think I'll try the little fish instead. They're more of a . . . challenge."

"Ha," I heard Jeremy snicker. "I knew it."

"Go for it," Brad said. He opened the jar and tossed me a tiny dried-up fish. "But aim straight for the eye."

I took the tiny fish between my fingers. Then Brad carefully handed me a hook.

Aim for the eye, I told myself as I brought the hook closer to the fish. "Aim for the eye. . . ."

Then . . .

"Eeek!" Jeremy squeaked.

It was just a dumb joke. But I screamed and

dropped the little fish on my leg. I jerked my leg—and knocked over the pail of worms. The worms took off across the deck.

I groaned as everyone ran to scoop them up. Then I sat down on a coil of rope and buried my face in my hands.

"Cheer up," a voice said. "You've made the worms very happy."

I looked up and saw Devon Benjamin smiling at me with those big green eyes.

"You think?" I asked.

"Sure," Devon said. "Wouldn't you rather be on deck than in the belly of some fish?"

Then Devon gave a little wave and joined the worm rescue.

What a nice guy, I thought. And so cute!

After Sid, Brad, and the campers scooped up most of the worms, all eyes turned to me.

"Wow!" I said with a nervous laugh. "Slippery little guys, aren't they?"

And, Diary, that was just the beginning! I'd tell you what happened when I went fishing, but the boys are outside slipping gummy worms under my door.

Not funny!

Two of a Kind Diaries

Dear Diary,

I'm back and writing to you from the porch this time. I don't want to write in my room with Ashley around, because this is going to be all about her.

Diary, Ashley's adventures in bait-hooking were bad enough. But when it came time to fish she went over the top. Literally!

After we got the hang of the fishing rods, Brad told us to drop our lines in the water. We all expected to get a bite right away. Instead we waited. And waited . . .

Then suddenly—

"I've got a bite!" Ashley cried out. From the way her fishing pole was bending, I could tell she wasn't kidding.

"Reel in the line!" Brad shouted.

"Okay!" Ashley said. She gritted her teeth as she tugged at the pole. "This fish is really big!"

We all ran over to help, but Ashley pushed us away.

"Stand back!" she cried. "I'm bringing this one in by myself!"

"Okay, Ashley," Brad called. "Reel it in as you

24

step back slowly. And make sure you don't grip too hard."

We all watched as Ashley did exactly what Brad said.

"Maybe it's a barracuda," Elise said.

"Or a swordfish," Justin said.

"Nah," Jeremy said. "I'll bet it's a shark!"

"Shark?" Ashley cried.

Her pole jerked hard. Ashley held on—then screamed as she went flying over the rail—and into the ocean!

"Twin overboard!" Cheryl yelled. "Twin overboard!"

Everyone ran to the rail and looked over. We all wore life vests, so Ashley didn't go under. But she probably wished she had. Her  face was red as a lobster from the embarrassment!

"Let that be a lesson, guys," Brad said after we pulled Ashley back in. "Never refuse help when reeling in a big fish."

Ashley gazed over the rail at her fishing pole floating out to sea in a ripple of currents.

"There it goes," she said. "My catch of the day."

"Oh, well," I said. "If it was a shark, you wouldn't want it anyway."

Ashley sighed and walked away.

I was going to remind her about our bet, but I changed my mind. She looked too upset. And I have to give her credit for trying.

That's it for now, Diary. Mrs. Clare just clued us in on a marshmallow roast on the beach. A marshmallow roast! I guess this is more like regular camp than I thought. See ya!

Chapter 4

Tuesday

Dear Diary,

The moment I woke up I knew it was the first day of scuba instruction. Probably because I had nightmares about it all night!

By the time I went down for breakfast I couldn't eat a thing. My stomach was already full—with butterflies!

"After breakfast we'll meet at the pool, where you'll suit up and get your scuba equipment," Jenny said. "We'll have our first classroom instruction later in the day."

"Scuba! Scuba! Scuba!" everyone yelled.

I yelled too just so Mary-Kate would think I was psyched.

When we filed into the pool area, Jenny handed out diving suits.

"Oh, none for me," Phoebe said. "I'm Phoebe Cahill. And I'm here to write my article for the *White Oak Acorn*."

Jenny looked confused. She looked at her list of students. "It says here that you're scheduled for scuba diving," she said. "All campers must participate."

Phoebe's eyes popped open behind her green-rimmed glasses. She clutched her reporter pad and pencil tightly.

"What?" Phoebe cried. "But I'm not cut out for sports! I'm more the intellectual type."

"Then you'll do great on the written test!" Jenny said with a smile. "And you can write all about your adventures in scuba for the paper."

"Phoebe! Phoebe! Phoebe!" everyone cheered.

Phoebe groaned and grabbed her diving suit. I knew exactly how she felt.

We put on our suits in the dressing rooms. They were tight and black and slick.

I looked around for Ross, but my eyes landed on Devon. He wasn't making seal noises like all the other boys. He looked calm and cool in his diving suit. And still very cute.

I gave my head a shake. What was I thinking? Ross was my boyfriend—and he was standing only a few feet away!

"Look!" Elise interrupted my thoughts. "That must be the equipment."

Shore Thing

I looked to see where Elise was pointing. There were racks and racks of tubes, belts, and masks.

"That's not scuba gear," Phoebe cried. "Those are instruments of torture!"

Jenny clapped her hands for attention.

"Listen up," she called out. "I want you all to see how a diver looks when he's ready to jump into the ocean."

The door to the boys' dressing room swung open. We all laughed as Jeremy stepped out in full scuba gear.

"Here's Jeremy modeling the equipment you'll need for your first dive," Jenny said.

Jeremy pretended to twirl like a supermodel.

"You'll all get a tank of compressed air," Jenny began. "A second-stage regulator and mouthpiece, a face mask, two submersible gauges—one to measure depth, the other to see how much air you have left in your tank—"

You mean it could run out? I thought.

"You'll also wear a weight belt to help you stay under," Jenny went on. "And fins on your feet to help propel you underwater."

Jeremy held up one foot and fell over.

"You're already wearing your wet suits. They help prevent hypothermia," Jenny said as Jeremy stood up. "Hypothermia is when your body temperature drops drastically."

"Are we diving in the Arctic?" Cheryl joked.

"No," Jenny said. "But the wet suit will also prevent cuts and scrapes underwater."

I gulped hard. Too much information!

"With the basic equipment a qualified diver can safely remain underwater for anywhere from a few minutes to two hours," Jenny said. "Any questions?"

I was dying to ask if my eyes would pop, but I didn't.

As Jenny passed out the masks, she mentioned all the great stuff we'd find under the sea once we had our certificates—bright pink coral, neon-colored fish, and underwater plants. We would

even borrow underwater cameras to take pictures.

"First we'll fit ourselves with the masks," Jenny said. "Just to get the feeling."

My heart raced as I struggled with the mask. I couldn't even get it over my head. Ross saw me panic and came over. He helped me adjust the straps and buckles. Soon the mask fit perfectly.

"All systems go!" Ross said.

I smiled under my mask and gave him a thumbs-up sign. My mask was on, and I didn't even freak.

A small step for scuba diving—a giant step for Ashley Burke!

I can't believe it, Diary. Maybe scuba diving won't be so bad after all.

And maybe I might even win this bet!

Dear Diary,

I thought I knew myself.

I like Rocky Road ice cream, the Chicago Cubs, and acting in school plays. I'm also good at sports.

At least until today . . .

"Here's your mask, Mary-Kate," Jenny said. "Now don't forget to adjust the buckle and straps. And make sure it's airtight."

"No problem," I said coolly. After all, I was the bathtub bubble-blowing champ of Chicago!

I stood next to Phoebe as we both adjusted our masks. Phoebe had hers on first.

"I can't breathe!" Phoebe gasped. She pointed to

her nose behind the scuba mask. "I can't breathe!"

"Breathe through your mouth," I told her.

"Oh," Phoebe said, taking a deep breath.

My mask adjusted, I pulled it over my face. For one second everything was fine.

Then something began to happen. It was as if the mask was closing in on me. Strangling me. Smothering me!

I ripped the mask off my face and took a deep breath.

"Mary-Kate, what's wrong?" Jenny asked.

"Nothing!" I gasped.

Jenny smiled. "It's okay to feel claustrophobic in your mask the first time," she said. "Lots of people do."

"I just had to sneeze," I said quickly. "And who wants to sneeze inside a scuba mask? Too gross!"

As Jenny walked away I glanced at Ashley. She was wearing her mask and looking totally cool.

Something was wrong with this picture. Ashley was the one who was supposed to be flipping out—not me!

Luckily class was over right after the masks. We changed into our regular clothes and headed back to our rooms for a mid-day break.

Ashley stuck around with Ross. I could see her

chattering on and on about our "awesome" scuba lesson.

I went into my room and plopped down on my bed. I closed my eyes and took a deep breath.

The next time you put on a mask, you'll be fine, I told myself. There's nothing scary about scuba diving—

Knock! Knock!

I opened the door and saw Phoebe.

"Mary-Kate!" Phoebe said. "Where's Ashley? I need to talk to her!"

"She's with Ross," I said. "What's up?"

Phoebe walked past me and sat on Ashley's bed. She shook her head.

"It's my article!" she said. "How can I write about scuba diving when all I can think of is two weeks of physical torture?"

"You'll get the hang of it," I said.

"How can I?" Phoebe cried. "The closest I've ever come to going underwater was looking in the fish tank in my dentist's office."

I sat down next to Phoebe. Then suddenly—

"Ow!" I said. Something hard was tucked under Ashley's blanket.

I pulled it out. It was Ashley's book, *The Worst That Can Happen.* "It's that dumb book!" I groaned.

"What book?" Phoebe asked. She picked it up and read the title. Then she began to flip through it.

"Wow," Phoebe said. "Did you know that building a snowman can freeze your hands?"

She kept flipping through the pages.

"Oh, no," Phoebe said. "There's a whole chapter on scuba diving. Did you know you could get something called compression sickness? Air embolism? Physical exhaustion?"

I blinked. Somehow the book didn't seem so funny anymore.

"What else?" I gulped.

"Injuries from marine life—" Phoebe gulped.

"Next chapter!" I urged.

Phoebe turned the page. Her jaw dropped.

"Mary-Kate!" she said. "Did you know that baby alligators can swim up through drains? And toilets?"

"I don't think I want to hear anymore," I said. We both jumped when we heard Ashley out in the hall.

"Don't tell Ashley we were reading her book," I

begged Phoebe. "I don't want her to know that I got scared."

"I promise," Phoebe said. "But it's okay to be scared, Mary-Kate."

That was easy for her to say. She doesn't have a major bet to win!

Chapter 5

Wednesday

Hi, Diary!

When I woke up this morning I was actually looking forward to our next scuba lesson. Imagine that!

Today we wore our bathing suits and got to try out our compressed air tanks. Mine wasn't as heavy as I thought it would be. And I had no trouble breathing under the shallow water of the pool.

"And now for a surprise," Jenny said after we practiced breathing. "We're going to play a game of dive and retrieve."

Jenny explained that we would be split up into teams of two. Then we would dive into the pool and pick up colorful weights under the water.

"Our first team will be Summer and Justin," Jenny called out. "Our second team will be Seth and Cheryl. . . ."

I glanced over at Mary-Kate. I know she's my twin, but I didn't want to team up with her. She would only show off and remind me about our bet!

"I hope they team us up," Ross whispered to me.

"Me, too!" I said.

"Our third team will be Ashley and Devon!" Jenny called out.

Shore Thing

Devon. Not Ross. I know I should have felt a little bad about it, but teaming up with Devon was going to be fun. I just knew it.

Jenny dropped the first weight in the pool. Then she signaled for Summer and Justin to dive. Everyone cheered as they swam underwater to search for it.

"This is cool," Devon said to me.

I glanced at Devon. He was looking at me through his long, silky black eyelashes.

"Yeah," I said slowly. "Way cool."

As we waited for our turn, Devon told me all about his adventures in scuba. He'd even gone diving in Hawaii!

"What was the neatest thing you ever saw under the sea?" I asked Devon.

"Once I saw something shiny on the sea floor," Devon explained. "It turned out to be an ancient Spanish coin."

"Wow!" I said.

Cheryl and Seth swam up with the bright blue weight. Then it was our turn.

"I might not be too good at this," I told Devon as we walked to the pool.

"You'll be great," Devon said. "Stick with me."

Jenny gave us the signal, and we dove into the pool. The weight belt around my waist helped me to stay under. I tried to keep calm as I breathed through my mouthpiece.

Devon pointed to the blue weight. We flapped our flippers and swam toward the weight. Our hands touched as we reached for it at the same time.

That's when it happened. My heart began to flutter and my head felt like it was in the clouds.

No—it wasn't decompression sickness. It was the same feeling I had when I first met Ross Lambert!

The next thing I felt was a pang of guilt. I mean— what if I'm actually falling for another boy?

Dear Diary,

I could sure use a dish of Rocky Road ice cream today. No. Make that a whole container!

When I found out we'd have our second scuba class today, my stomach did a triple flip. Would I totally choke like yesterday? And if I did—would Ashley notice?

Standing next to Phoebe didn't help either.

"I heard we're diving in the pool today!" Phoebe

whispered. "Do you remember what Ashley's book said about diving?"

I didn't want to hear about it again. I put my mask on, and this time I managed to keep it on. I also did pretty well with my oxygen tank. Until I had a horrible thought . . .

"Hey, Phoebe," I whispered. "What happens if you fall backwards on the tank?"

"Forget that," Phoebe whispered back. "What happens if these tanks explode?"

Explode? That did it!

"Jenny?" I blurted. "I can't finish the class today!"

"Why not, Mary-Kate?" Jenny asked.

"My stomach!" I said, grabbing my middle. "It must have been that kiwi oatmeal I had this morning!"

Jenny looked concerned. "Then you'd better go back to your room," she said. "But have someone walk you back."

Ashley raised her hand. "I'll go with her," she said.

"No!" Phoebe shouted. "I will! I will! I will!"

Phoebe and I dashed out of the pool area. We

leaned against the fence and sighed with relief.

"Good thinking, Mary-Kate," Phoebe said. "You got us *both* out of this class!"

But I was still worried. I mean, how could I go from being super-jock to super-chicken in just a few days?

Diary, help!

Chapter 6

Thursday

Dear Diary,

My drama class training is really paying off. This morning everyone believed me when I said I was still sick.

Everyone except Ashley.

"So how are you really feeling, Mary-Kate?" Ashley asked. She tilted her head as she watched me in bed.

"Awwwwwful!" I moaned. "My head is stuffed, my nose is running, and my head is pounding!"

"That's weird," Ashley said. "Yesterday you told Jenny that your stomach hurt."

"My stomach hurts too!" I blurted. "The pain's just moving up, that's all!"

Ashley sighed. She pulled a blouse over her bathing suit and headed to the door.

"Well, you'll be missing our third scuba class," she said. "And there's only three more until the certification test."

As if I didn't know!

"Anyhow I'll look in on you later," Ashley went on. "After scuba class. After I blow everybody away with my incredible diving skills!"

I rolled my eyes. Ashley was busting my chops about the bet. And she still didn't know how scared I was!

The door closed and I was alone. I stared up at the ceiling and noticed a small spider web.

Spiders, I thought. I grabbed Ashley's book and opened to the chapter on spiders.

"'A bite from a tarantula can cause instant death,'" I read to myself. "Death?"

I ran for the door. I was about to call for help when I stopped short.

"I've got to get a grip," I told myself. "Especially if I'm going to win this bet!"

But first I had to deal with a serious case of scuba-phobia!

"I know!" I told myself. "I'll practice blowing bubbles in the bathtub. If I could do it when I was five, I can do it now!"

I changed into my bathing suit. Then I grabbed the mask and carried it to the girls shower room. Next to the two shower stalls was a white bathtub with iron legs. I turned on the cool water and filled it up.

"Okay," I said, stepping into the tub. "Here goes."

I slipped the mask over my face. I tried not to panic as I dunked under the water.

Cool, I thought as I peered through my scuba mask. I could see every tiny crack in the porcelain. Even the silver drain seemed to sparkle.

I began to relax and blow bubbles. Until I remembered what Phoebe said about bathtub drains . . .

Alligators! I thought. Baby alligators swim up through drains and toilets!

"Ahhh!" I jumped up and pulled off my mask.

A knock on the door made me jump.

"Is somebody in there?" Mrs. Clare called.

"No, Mrs. Clare," I called back. "Nobody here but us chickens!"

Dear Diary,

Call the newspaper because I did it! Today I won a contest of underwater steal the bacon!

"You see?" Devon told me after instruction. "You never know what you can do until you try!"

I knew I liked Devon Benjamin. And I wanted to hang out with him—but how could I? Especially since Ross and I had planned to spend lots of time together. And Ross was my boyfriend . . .

"Sid said he'd drive a bunch of us to town after lunch," Ross said. "How about it?"

"Sure!" I said.

I was hoping Devon would sign up for the trip, but he didn't. Instead it was just Ross, Elise, Justin, and me.

When we reached the town it turned out to be only three blocks long. There were small shops and huts selling boating tours, seafood, and souvenirs.

Ross and I went inside this cool shop that sold sunglasses, postcards, stuffed toy alligators, and loads of T-shirts. But while Ross looked at ships in bottles, I was on the lookout for Devon Benjamin.

Maybe he borrowed the camp bike and rode to town. Maybe he had to buy a present for his mother. Or maybe for his sister, if he has one. Naturally he doesn't have a girlfriend! He couldn't! He wouldn't! Don't even go there!

But just as I was about to buy some saltwater taffy, I saw something awesome dangling in front of my eyes!

It was a beautiful coral choker!

I spun around and saw Ross. He was holding the pink-and-white necklace and grinning.

"For me?" I asked.

Ross nodded with a big smile on his face.

"Put it on," he urged.

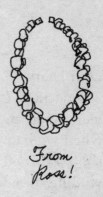

From Ross!

I walked over to a mirror framed with shells. I hooked the choker around my neck. It looked great. But deep inside I felt awful. How could I accept a gift from Ross when just a few minutes ago I was hoping that Devon would show up?

"Thanks, Ross," was all I could say. "It's beautiful."

Oh, Diary! Why does Devon have to be so cute?

Chapter 7

Friday

Dear Diary,

I decided I am not going to let my fears spoil my fun. So this morning when we had our photography workshop, I turned my attention to the art of capturing wildlife. Besides, what could be dangerous about taking pictures?

Keith showed us slides of birds and tropical fish. The colors were incredibly bright and beautiful.

But then a slide appeared of a snake curled up on a rock.

"You got that from a magazine, right?" Summer asked. "Like *National Geometric*?"

"*National Geographic*, Summer!" Cheryl groaned.

"No way!" Keith said. "One of the campers from last year snapped this shot. Right near the swamp."

"Aren't most snakes—poisonous?" I asked.

"Some of them are," Keith said. "You'll learn all about them in marine biology."

I nodded. Then I felt Phoebe tap my shoulder.

"Remember to check out the chapter on snakes later!" she whispered.

Anyway, Diary, I've got to fly. Camp Coral Reef is throwing us a pizza party tonight in the rec room.

Shore Thing

Sure, I'm still worried about scuba diving. But extra cheese and pepperoni always makes things easier.

Ciao!

Dear Diary,

We just had the most awesome pizza party and I am stuffed to the gills! (That's a Florida Keys fish joke. Everyone's saying it.)

My favorite cheese and mushroom pie was there. But I had to be convinced that the droopy green stuff on one was spinach—not seaweed!

When the local DJ played a slow song, I danced with Ross. A few months ago I would have been floating on the moon, but tonight I felt totally guilty. The coral necklace Ross gave me seemed to make me itch.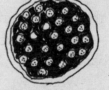

Diary, is there a way for a boy to know that you MIGHT like someone else? Do your eyes twitch? Do you smell weird? Do you eat your pizza differently? I sure hope not!

The slow song ended and Ross and I walked over to the chips and dip. As I chewed on a chip with guacamole I looked around the room. No Devon.

"Want some pineapple punch, Ashley?" Ross asked.

"Sure," I said. He walked over to the drinks table and I wandered over to the window. I looked out and saw the moon glimmering on the ocean.

I slipped out the back door onto the porch. Guess who was there leaning against a rail—Devon!

"Hi," I said, trying to ignore my racing heart.

Devon looked back and smiled. "Hey!"

I leaned over the rail next to him. Not too close.

"Great party!" I said.

"It would be better if they didn't play so much 4-You!" Devon groaned.

I was hoping I heard wrong. 4-You is my favorite band.

"What's wrong with 4-You?" I asked.

Devon shrugged. "They sound like they're in pain," he said.

I wanted to argue but didn't. So Devon doesn't like 4-You. Well, nobody's perfect!

"We're going canoeing tomorrow," Devon said. "I saw it on the schedule."

"I've never gone canoeing," I said. "What's it like?"

"It's great!" Devon said. "Maybe we can share a canoe, and I'll show you the ropes."

Shore Thing

Share a canoe? I was so excited I couldn't speak. I pictured myself in a canoe with Devon. Gliding over crystal clear water under the bright Florida stars—

"Ashley?" Ross's voice interrupted my thoughts.

"Huh?" I spun around. Ross was standing at the back door. He was holding two cups of pineapple punch.

"Oh, hi, Ross!" I said. I hurried to him and pulled him back into the rec room.

"I couldn't find you," he said. "Let's finish this punch and dance again. They're playing some more 4-You!"

"Great!" I said.

I had a feeling Ross didn't suspect anything. But that only made me feel guiltier!

Chapter 8

Saturday

Dear Diary,

Today at breakfast I sat between Mary-Kate and Ross. Out of the corner of my eye I saw Devon eating a corn muffin with guava jelly. Did he remember what he had said about the canoe trip today? I hoped so!

"Think of this canoe trip as practice," Brad said after breakfast. "For the race in a few days!"

"Race?" Excited whispers filled the dining room.

"I'll explain the race later," Brad said. "Are there any questions about today's trip?"

"Where are we going to canoe?" I asked. Down a crystal clear stream? A quiet lake? A babbling brook?

"The swamp!" Brad answered with a smile. "Where else are you going to see tropical trees, birds, and insects?"

Insects? I was hoping Mary-Kate didn't see the big lump in my throat!

Mrs. Clare instructed us to pack our backpacks with sandwiches, juice, and bug lotion. Then we filed into the camp minibus where I sat next to Mary-Kate.

"I am so totally psyched," Mary-Kate said. "I

hope we do see some alligators. Lots of them!"

"Well, I hope we see snakes," I said. "A big mamba!"

"What's that?" Mary-Kate asked.

"Something poisonous," I said. "I read about it in my *Worst That Can Happen* book. Chapter five."

"Nuh-uh!" Mary-Kate said, shaking her head. "Snakes are in chapter seven—" She bit her lip.

I was about to ask her how she knew that when Brad stopped the bus. We filed out and saw canoes and oars lined up on the muddy bank of the swamp.

We stood and stared at the brownish green water. Sticking out of the muck were swamp grass and gnarly tree branches that looked like claws. Curtains of moss dripped from trees like dark green slime.

"I think I saw this in a movie," Jeremy said.

"*The African Queen*?" Phoebe asked.

"No," Jeremy said. "*The Creature from the Black Lagoon*!"

"Okay, gang!" Brad called. He clapped his hands. "Grab your backpacks and team up in groups of three!"

Phoebe grabbed Mary-Kate's arm. Mary-Kate grabbed Elise.

"So are we a team or what?" a voice asked.

I turned and saw Devon grinning at me.

"You bet!" I said, smiling back. But then I saw Ross walking toward us. "You, me—and Ross Lambert!"

Brad gave us a canoeing demonstration. We practiced holding our oars. Then we dragged our canoes into the swamp. Bullfrogs boomed from nearby islands and branches.

"Smooth sailing all the way!" Devon said. He took hold of the canoe and jumped in the back.

Ross looked disappointed. I think *he* wanted to steer. Instead he took the front and I took the middle.

Paddling our canoe down the swamp was like pushing through thick, sticky oatmeal. But as Devon pointed out pelicans, horseshoe crabs, and a few deer on the bank, the swamp began to look less scary and more exciting!

"The roots growing out of the water are called mangroves," Devon explained. "We have to be careful not to get stuck in one."

"Hey!" Ross called out. "What's that?"

I turned. Ross was pointing to a huge turtle sitting on a nearby island.

Shore Thing

The turtle blinked at us as we steered closer to the island. He was about the size of Mary-Kate's basketball.

"Watch this," Ross said. He leaned out of the canoe and hoisted the turtle into the boat.

"What are you doing?" I cried.

"Taking him back to camp," Ross said. "I want to show the guys what we found."

"You better put him back, Ross," Devon warned. "Turtles can be dangerous."

Ross didn't listen. He placed the turtle on the floor of our canoe—right in front of me!

"Here, Ashley!" Ross laughed. "A souvenir!"

As I began to slide away from it, the turtle thrust his head out and grabbed hold of my sneaker with his mouth!

"Ahhh!" I shouted. "Get him off meeee!" I shrieked, shaking my foot.

Ross pulled at the tur-
tle. He even tapped on
his shell. But that turtle
didn't budge!

"Watch out!" Devon
warned. He reached out and grabbed my ankle. With a swift jerk he yanked the sneaker off my foot!

Carefully Devon pried the turtle's jaw from my

sneaker. Then he placed the turtle back into the swamp.

"A snapping turtle," Ross said, shrugging. "Who knew?"

I was so grateful I leaned over and gave Devon a big hug. Big mistake!

Dear Diary,

I may be snug in my bed now but just hours ago I was in the middle of a mucky, yucky swamp!

The minute Phoebe, Elise, and I stepped into our canoe I knew there'd be trouble. . . .

"Stop shaking the canoe!" Elise demanded.

"How can I stop shaking the canoe when I can't stop shaking myself?" Phoebe cried.

Phoebe was dressed in vintage army camouflage.

She wore a 1940s hat on her head with a net to cover her face.

"No way am I getting a mosquito bite," Phoebe told us. "I read all about malaria in that book."

"What book?" Elise asked.

I spun around and glared at Phoebe.

"Um—*Little Women*!" Phoebe said quickly.

"They get malaria?" Elise cried.

"No!" Phoebe said. "I mean yes. In the sequel!"

Our canoe drifted through swamp grass and soupy water. I sat in the bow of the canoe, which meant I saw everything first. Every bug. Every snake. Every horseshoe crab.

The swamp got narrower as we paddled. "This hanging moss is gross!" I said, brushing it aside. "And what's that glittery stuff coming up?"

"Glittery?" Elise gasped. "Where?"

Elise loved anything glitter. But as we got closer, I was pretty sure she wouldn't love this.

I gasped as layers and layers of spider webs stretched over our heads. With big yellow and black spiders!

"Ahhggggh!" Phoebe cried.

We ducked, but it was no use. The spider webs seemed to dip lower and lower. They practically brushed our heads!

"Little Miss Muffet was right," I shouted. "I'm out of here!"

"Where are you going?" Phoebe demanded.

I looked around. There was a tiny, mossy island about fifteen feet away.

"There!" I said.

"I'm right behind you!" Phoebe declared.

Phoebe and I swung our legs over the canoe.

"Stop!" Elise shouted. "You can't swim in the swamp!"

"Why not?" I asked.

"Hel-lo?" Elise asked. "Haven't you ever heard of alligators?"

Phoebe and I both froze.

"Alligators?" we shouted at the same time.

We swung our legs back into the canoe.

"Now get a grip, will you?" Elise demanded.

I gritted my teeth as we paddled on. The spider webs began to thin out. And we made it safely to the other side.

And not a moment too soon.

Later on the bus, Ashley asked me how the ride went.

I was dying to tell Ashley the truth. That I wasn't as brave as I said. That I was probably a bigger wimp than she was. And that I wish I never, ever made that stupid bet.

But I didn't.

"Great!" I told her. "Can't wait for that race!"

Now Ashley is busy brushing her teeth, so I'm going to check out her *The Worst That Can Happen* book.

I want to see what it says about mosquito bites.

And malaria!

Chapter 9

Sunday

Dear Diary,

You are not going to believe what happened today.

I spent all night scratching these mosquito bites I got in the swamp yesterday. So the minute the sun came up, I reached for Ashley's book. I flipped through it quietly under the covers.

"Malaria," I said. "What does it say about malaria?"

I found malaria in the book and read to myself. Phoebe was right. Malaria *was* carried by mosquitoes!

"The symptoms of malaria are severe headaches, chills, and extremely high fever . . ."

My head began to ache. I broke out into a cold sweat. And from what I saw—my skin was pretty red!

"Mary-Kate—what are you doing?" Ashley's voice demanded.

I gasped and popped my head out of the covers. "I don't feel good," I blurted out.

"What do you have now?" Ashley asked.

"Malaria!" I shrieked.

"What?" Ashley cried. She ran over to my bed

and felt my head. "You *are* kind of warm."

"I knew it!" I groaned. "It's been nice knowing you, Ashley. You can have my 4-You CDs. And give my Chicago Cubs jerseys to my roommate, Campbell! And tell Dad—"

"Mary-Kate!" Ashley said. "You might just have a cold. What makes you think it's malaria?"

"Because," I said, shoving Ashley's book deeper under the covers, "the mosquitoes in that swamp were the size of turkeys!"

"Okay," Ashley said. She began to look concerned. "I'll tell the counselors. Maybe they can get the camp doctor to come here."

Ashley pulled on a pair of shorts and a T-shirt. She was about to leave when she turned toward the night table.

Big ugly Mosquito

"Did you see my book?" she asked. "It was on the night table last night."

"Your book?" I asked. "Um. No. I didn't see it."

Ashley shook her head and left. I lay in bed during breakfast and stared at the ceiling.

Maybe having malaria won't be so bad, I thought. I would get lots of attention. And I wouldn't have to do any more camp activities.

Shore Thing

I wouldn't even have to take the scuba certification test—

A knock on the door interrupted my thoughts.

"Come in," I called.

A woman with dark hair opened my door. "Hello, Mary-Kate," she said with a smile. "I'm Dr. Alvarez. I heard you're not feeling too well."

"Yes," I answered.

The doctor listened to my chest and popped a thermometer in my mouth. Then she examined my arms and legs. After all that she smiled again.

"You can tell me, Dr. Alvarez," I said. "I'm tough. At least I used to be."

"Tell you what?" Dr. Alvarez asked.

I took a deep breath. "That I have malaria!"

The doctor began to laugh.

"I'm sorry!" Dr. Alvarez said. "It's just that there is no malaria in Florida. You'd have to go all the way to Africa to catch that."

I plopped my head back on the pillow. I was never so relieved—and embarrassed—in my life.

"You do have a pretty bad sunburn, though," Dr. Alvarez said. "I recommend cold compresses and calamine lotion. Stay inside today. And use lots and lots of sunscreen tomorrow!"

The doctor gave me a pink bottle of calamine

lotion. Then I thanked her, and she left.

"Now there's only one more thing I have to do to feel better," I said to myself as I jumped out of bed. I reached under the covers and pulled out *The Worst That Can Happen.*

"I have to stop reading this stupid book!"

Dear Diary,

Good news. Mary-Kate does not have malaria!

"I'm glad you're okay," I told Mary-Kate when I checked up on her before scuba class.

"Me, too," Mary-Kate said. "But the doctor wants me to stay out of the sun today. I'm just so upset that I have to miss scuba."

I looked at Mary-Kate with that big grin on her face. She didn't look very upset to me.

"Well, you can't keep missing scuba diving," I said. "We're going to take our scuba certification test in four days. Remember our bet?"

"Don't worry!" Mary-Kate shrugged. "The bet's still on—and I'm going to win."

I tried to stay away from Devon today. After that snapping turtle incident yesterday, I have a hunch Ross knows I like him. At breakfast this morning, Ross barely took his nose out of his oatmeal.

"What's the matter?" I asked.

"You didn't have to hug him," he muttered, glaring at Devon across the room.

"That was just a friendly hug," I insisted. "It didn't mean anything."

But I don't think Ross believed me.

"This afternoon there'll be a choice of activities," Sid announced during lunch. "You can either take a photography workshop on the beach or see a movie on sharks at the marine biology center."

Sid asked for a show of hands. I watched Devon raise his hand for photography. Then I saw Ross raise his hand for the shark movie.

"Ashley," Sid said. "You have to choose an activity."

My head was spinning. The last thing I wanted to see was a movie about sharks. But if I chose photography, Ross would think I just wanted to hang out with Devon.

"What will it be, Ashley?" Sid asked.

"Mary-Kate!" I blurted. "I mean, my sister is stuck in her room today. I want to keep her company."

"Well, that's nice of you, Ashley," Sid said.

Diary, what else could I do?

So when everybody went off to their activities, I headed upstairs to our room.

"Mary-Kate?" I called softly as I opened the door. No answer. Mary-Kate was fast asleep.

I sat on the wicker chair and glanced out the window. The beach looked so inviting. Maybe I'd just take a little walk. No use wasting the sun, I thought.

I glanced back over at Mary-Kate, who was still in la-la land. Then I decided to go out.

And guess who I ran into on the beach. Keith and the photography workshop!

Keith had no problem with me joining in. He gave me a camera and told me that the pictures I took would develop before my eyes in just seconds. After a quick lesson on loading film we began snapping away.

Elise looked for starfish. Jeremy was on the hunt for giant water bugs. (Yuck!) And for a moment I forgot about Devon and searched the beach for exotic wildlife.

"Ew!" I said. I pointed to something scurrying across the sand. "What's that thing?"

 "It's a sand crab!" Keith said with a grin. "And he'd make a great shot. Don't you think?"

I ran after it and snapped a picture.

Keith was right. Everything looked great

through a camera lens. Even something with a million legs!

I was having a great time taking pictures of tropical flowers, pelicans—even an awesome white cockatoo up in a tree. Until I spotted the most beautiful creature of all—Devon Benjamin!

Sure, we talked a bit. And he hung around while I took wildlife photos.

So can I help it if Devon just happens to be in the background?

Dear Diary,

I know I already wrote to you today, Diary, but have I got news about Ashley!

After a nice snooze I was eating a late lunch in the dining room. My sunburn had faded a bit and didn't hurt so much. And I was feeling braver after throwing out that stupid book!

"I am going to ace that scuba test," I told myself.

"Scuba! Scuba!" Taco squawked. His cage was behind me but I knew he had his eye on the cracker in my conch chowder!

"There you are, Mary-Kate!" Ashley said as she rushed into the dining room. She was holding something in her hands and looking very excited.

"Where were you?" I asked my sister.

"Wildlife photography!" Ashley announced. She smiled as she laid her pictures out on the table.

I studied the shots. The first few were of this crabby looking critter. The rest were a little more—human!

"Half of these pictures are of Devon!" I exclaimed.

Ashley's eyes opened wide. "Devon who?" she blurted.

"Devon Benjamin!" I said. I pointed to the pictures one by one. "Devon waving from a sand dune. Devon taking a picture of a cockatoo. Devon sticking his foot in the ocean and pretending he's cold. Devon, Devon, Devon!"

"Shhh!" Ashley hissed, grabbing my arm.

"Ow!" I cried. "Sunburn!"

"Sorry!" Ashley said. "But all those pictures of Devon are just a coincidence."

"I don't think so," I said. "I can tell you like him because you got that look on your face when you laid out his pictures," I said.

"Look?" Ashley demanded. "What look?"

"The faraway look you always have when you're in love," I said. "Like you're looking at a sunset!"

Ashley's shoulders dropped. Call it a twin thing

but I knew she was about to come clean.

"Okay!" Ashley cried. "I do have a crush on Devon. But whatever you do, you have to promise not to tell Ross!"

"I promise," I said. Then I smiled and began to sing softly. "Ashley loves Devon. Ashley loves Devon."

"Mary-Kate!" Ashley complained. She bit into one of my rolls. "By the way, Mary-Kate. Did you notice that I'm acing all of the camp activities?"

"That's nice," I said.

"Which reminds me," Ashley said slowly. "This is the fourth scuba class you missed today. And yesterday after the canoe trip your knees were shaking so much you could barely get out of the canoe. What was that all about?"

"So I was suffering from seasickness!" I blurted.

"Whatever," Ashley said. She began to collect her pictures. "I'm bringing these back to my room. And remember when you see Ross, don't tell him I spent the day with Devon. He thinks I was keeping you company."

Aha! Now I know Ashley's little secret.

And if I'm not more careful—she's going to find out mine!

Chapter 10

Monday

Dear Diary,

The most awful thing happened at breakfast this morning. And it's all Mary-Kate's fault!

"Hey, everybody!" Jeremy called when Mary-Kate and I came down for breakfast. "Ashley has a new boyfriend!"

I felt my legs stiffen.

"What are you talking about?" I demanded.

"As if you didn't know!" Summer giggled.

"Ashley loves Devon, Ashley loves Devon," Jeremy began to sing.

"Ashley loves Devon!" Taco screeched. "Arrrk!"

The table began to snicker. Ross's mouth was a thin grim line as he looked at me from the corner of his eye.

"Devon is a hottie! Devon is a hottie!" Taco screeched. "Arrk!"

"I taught him how to say that!" Jeremy laughed.

I pulled Mary-Kate aside. "I told you not to tell!"

"I didn't!" Mary-Kate insisted.

"Then who did?" I snapped. "We were the only ones in the dining room when I told you!"

"I don't have a clue!" Mary-Kate shrugged.

"Yeah, sure," I snapped. I was going to sit down next to Ross but he was already leaving the dining room.

"Ross, wait up!" I said out in the hall.

Ross spun around. "Doesn't that necklace mean anything to you?" he asked.

"Yes!" I said, touching the coral choker. "You know how much I like you, Ross."

What I didn't say was that I liked Devon, too. But I didn't have a chance. Ross turned and walked away.

It's not fair, Diary! A person can like two flavors of ice cream—even three—and get away with it. So why can't I like two boys?

Dear Diary,

Let's set the record straight. I did not blab Ashley's secret. But does Ashley believe me? Noooo!

And boy—was she mad. After breakfast she dragged me all the way back to our room and let me have it.

"This is your way of getting even, isn't it?" Ashley demanded. "Because I'm winning your stupid bet and you're starting to wimp out!"

The words made my toes twist.

"Wimp out?" I asked. "What do you mean?"

"I'd tell you," Ashley said. She pointed to her watch. "But from this moment on we are not speaking."

"Give me a break!" I groaned. Ashley stomped out of the room.

I sat down on my bed and sighed. There was no way I could prove to Ashley that I didn't blab. But now that I felt braver, I could probably learn to scuba dive.

I changed into my red bathing suit. Then I marched out to the beach. Ashley and some of the campers were playing volleyball. Others were snorkeling in the ocean with Brad and Jenny.

"Mary-Kate!" Phoebe said. She was sitting on a beach blanket and shaking her head. "I'm trying to write about scuba diving, but all I can think of is sharks."

"Sharks!" I threw back my head and headed for the ocean. "I laugh in the face of sharks. Ha!"

"Mary-Kate?" Phoebe asked. "Where are you going?"

"For a swim!" I told her. "The sea is our friend, you know. Ask the Little Mermaid!"

Shore Thing

The waves crashed around my legs as I walked into the ocean. The water felt nice and cool against my sunburn. I walked deeper and deeper.

When I was in up to my waist I took a deep breath. I was about to dip myself when I saw something pink and shimmery on top of the water.

"Oooh," I thought. "That's beautiful." I stared at it as it floated closer and closer. . . .

"Watch out!" a voice shouted.

I felt a hand grip my shoulder. I spun around and saw Devon. "Get away from that!" he ordered.

Man O' War!

"Why?" I asked as we hurried to shore.

"That was a Man o' War!" Devon said. "The biggest, meanest jellyfish there is. You don't want to get stung by him!"

My knees shook. My heart raced. I wanted to thank Devon, but my mouth was as dry as sawdust.

Who am I kidding, Diary?

In three days we take the scuba certification test—and I can't even put my head underwater!

Chapter 11

Tuesday

Dear Diary,

This morning Ross wasn't talking to me. And I wasn't talking to Mary-Kate. How could I after she blabbed my secret all over camp?

"Cheryl," I said at breakfast. "Please tell Mary-Kate to pass the guava jelly."

Mary-Kate turned to Cheryl. "Tell Ashley it isn't guava," she said. "It's pineapple!"

"Tell her yourself," Cheryl complained. "I'm out of here." She picked up her tray and left.

Ross didn't speak to me all through scuba class or marine biology. I was feeling worse and worse. Ross never did anything bad to me. And now I've embarrassed him in front of the whole camp!

At least I didn't mean to.

During our mid-day break Devon asked me to go to town with him. I just wanted to get away—so I said yes.

We got permission from Sid to borrow the camp bikes. Then we peddled up the road to town. Just the two of us.

"How about some ice cream?" Devon asked as we chained our bikes to a fence.

"Cool!" I said. "I could go for mint chocolate chip in a waffle cone."

"Mint chocolate chip?" Devon cried. He wrinkled his nose and stuck out his tongue. "Yuck!"

I starred at him. Devon and I obviously had nothing in common.

Why would I like a boy who hates 4-You and mint-chocolate-chip ice cream?

Sure, Devon is cute. But there are lots of good-looking boys in the world. And only one Ross.

Ross loves 4-You and mint-chocolate-chip ice cream. And most important—he likes *me!*

"I *love* mint chocolate chip," I said firmly. "And I think I'll make mine a *double scoop!*"

Devon shrugged and ordered a vanilla cone for himself.

Vanilla? Boring!

Diary, now I have two goals: winning the bet and getting Ross back.

So wish me luck!

Dear Diary,

After seeing that Man o' War in the ocean yesterday I was happy to see the swimming pool again. I even managed to get into the pool with my mask and tank on.

I quickly dunked my head underwater.

"Maybe there's hope," I told Phoebe after I climbed out of the pool. "Maybe I'm not such a chicken after all."

"Speak for yourself," Phoebe wailed. "I still haven't gone underwater yet."

"Okay, you guys!" Jenny called. "I have a surprise for you. Tomorrow afternoon you'll finally get to dive in the ocean!"

I remembered the Man o' War and began to sweat.

What if it were waiting for me? What if I stepped on one of its babies and now it wants revenge?

I gave my head a shake. I had watched way too many movies on the Fright Channel!

"The ocean dive is all in preparation for your scuba test in two days," Jenny said.

"Scuba! Scuba! Scuba!" everyone cheered.

I glanced at Ashley cheering along.

"Look at her," I mumbled under my breath. "Miss Navy Seal."

Diary, this is more than I can take. Why am I suddenly the wuss and Ashley the superhero?

It's not just unfair—it's against the law of nature!

Chapter 12

Wednesday

Dear Diary,

When I woke up this morning the first thing I did was check my sunburn. It was a pale cotton-candy pink.

Not red enough to get me out of that ocean dive!

I could hear Ashley in the bathroom singing "Under the Sea" at the top of her lungs. To her, *The Worst That Can Happen* book is history. To me it's a constant reminder of things to come. *Disaster!*

Right after breakfast we suited up for the dive. Then we boarded Sid's special diving boat.

"Remember, divers!" Sid called as he sailed the boat out to sea. "If you find any sunken treasure I get a cut!"

"What if we find skeletons?" Jeremy called out.

Everyone laughed except Phoebe and me.

"Why don't they just make us walk the plank?" Phoebe groaned.

My stomach churned as the boat sailed farther and farther away from the shore. When it stopped after about a mile, Sid dropped an anchor. Then Jenny took over. She gave a talk about boat safety, then guided us to the diving platform.

"Now remember," Jenny said. "Breathe naturally

through your mouthpiece. That's the key."

My heart pounded as the campers jumped into the ocean one by one. Then it was my turn. I stood next to Jeremy on the platform and stared into the water.

"Go for it!" Jeremy said. He tapped my shoulder lightly. But I was so nervous I tumbled overboard!

I squeezed my eyes shut as I splashed into the water and began to sink. Water rushed all around me. I began to panic. But then I stopped falling and began to float.

Breathing through my mouthpiece I felt weightless. Almost as if I was on the moon!

My eyes popped open and I gasped. A school of neon fish swam past my mask. I looked around and saw electric-colored fish everywhere. Tiny bubbles floated around mountains of coral and forests of underwater plants.

Holy mackerel, I thought. *This is awesome!*

Summer and Justin waved to me under the water. Then the three of us followed a school of catfish around a coral peak. Jenny was right— scuba diving was like visiting a whole new world. By the time I swam back to the surface I felt empowered and totally exhilarated!

Diary—spread the word.

Mary-Kate Burke went deep sea diving and loved it.

And she is back in the game!

Dear Diary,

Bad news.

Getting Ross back is not going to be as easy as I thought.

Today I tried everything. I wore the coral choker he gave me. I smiled at him so much my face hurt. I even sat next to him on Sid's diving boat.

"Do you believe we're going scuba diving under the ocean?" I asked Ross as the boat sailed out.

"Hmmph," Ross said.

Try again.

"I'm so psyched that you're coming to Chicago, Ross," I said. "I'll show you the Sears Tower and we can even see a Cubs game if you'd like—"

"Who says I'm still coming to Chicago?" Ross grumbled.

Uh-oh.

"But, Ross," I said. "What about the 4-You concert? We were going together, remember?"

"Why don't you just go with Mr. Florida Tan?" Ross snapped. "Devon Benjamin?"

The boat jerked and so did my stomach. I glanced at Devon on the other side of the boat. He was busy putting on sunscreen and talking to Justin.

I turned to Ross. I had to set the record straight once and for all.

"Devon doesn't even like 4-You," I said firmly. "Besides, you're the one I want to go with. Because you're the guy I like!"

Ross stared straight ahead as he leaned on a life preserver. "You mean it?" he asked.

"Cross my heart and hope to die!" I said.

Ross broke into a smile.

"So will you come to Chicago this summer?" I asked.

"Maybe," Ross said.

"Maybe" wasn't as good as "yes." But it was better than "no"!

That was the last thing Ross said to me all day, but at least now I have hope. In fact, I even made up a list of reasons I want Ross back, so that I don't give up.

WHY I WANT ROSS BACK: He's nice. He makes me laugh. He's cute. He's a Gemini like me. He does an awesome impression of our headmistress, Mrs. Pritchard! He likes 4-You and mint-chocolate-chip ice cream.

Best of all, he really likes me. And I'd better work fast if I want to keep it that way!

Chapter 13

Thursday

Dear Diary,
 Today there were no activities, so we could all spend the day studying for our scuba certificate test.

 Before lunch, I saw Ashley cramming with Cheryl on a beach blanket. I wanted to join them but knew better. Ashley would just tell me to "be like an egg and beat it!"

 I went to my room and tried to study buoyancy compensators and second-stage regulators. But something was missing. Not my notes. Not even the flannel shirt I always wear when I study for a test.

 What was missing was Ashley!

 You see, ever since Ashley and I were in third grade we always studied together. And right before a test we would give each other our traditional good luck thumbs-up!

 I lay back on my bed and gave a big sigh.

 Why won't Ashley believe that I didn't blab her secret? And why can't this stupid fight be over once and for all?

 Tossing my scuba textbook aside I picked up my diary. I opened it to the last page and froze. It wasn't my diary—it was Ashley's!

"Whoops!" I tried to shut it. But my eyes became glued to a list called—WHY I WANT ROSS BACK.

"So Ashley still likes Ross!" I told myself as I read the list. "What do you know . . ."

I heard someone in the hall. Shutting the diary, I felt my heart pound. Ashley couldn't know I was reading her diary—even if it *was* by mistake!

"Fingerprints!" I hissed.

Grabbing a tissue, I rubbed the cover of the diary. But just as I was about to toss the tissue away I noticed a pile of pictures on the bottom of the wastebasket.

I shuffled through the pictures. They were Ashley's wildlife shots—the ones filled with Devon!

"So that's it," I said to myself. "Ashley is over Devon. Which is why she wants Ross back!"

Suddenly I had a brilliant idea. If I could help Ashley get Ross back, maybe she'd get over our fight!

I ran outside and looked for Ross. I found him swinging in a hammock behind the house.

"Hi, Ross!" I said.

Ross looked up from his scuba textbook.

"Hey, Mary-Kate," Ross said. He shifted over and made room for me to sit down. "What's up?"

I took a deep breath and got right to the point.

"Look, Ross," I said. "Ashley thinks you're great! She wants to be your girlfriend again."

Ross began to swing the hammock as he thought. "But what about Devon?" he asked. "What if Ashley still likes him?"

"Devon Shmevon!" I said. "If she likes him so much what are his pictures doing in the trash can?"

"Pictures?" Ross asked. "What pictures?"

"The pictures from the photography workshop," I explained. "I was sick that day, and you must have been at that shark movie."

Ross's smile turned into a big frown. What did I say?

"Ashley told me she wasn't going to that workshop," Ross said. "She said she was going to spend the whole afternoon with you."

My jaw dropped open. How could I forget that Ashley didn't want Ross to know?

"Ashley *was* going to spend the afternoon with me," I said quickly. "But I was fast asleep. So who can blame her for splitting?"

Ross got up from the hammock so fast that it

tipped back. I fell back on the ground with a THUNK.

"Where are you going?" I called out to Ross.

"To find Ashley," Ross called back. "And tell her my trip to Chicago is off. She *lied* to me!"

"Oh, noooo!" I groaned.

I lay on the ground and stared up at the puffy white clouds. All I wanted to do was make things better.

And now I had made things worse!

Dear Diary,

Motor-mouth Mary-Kate Burke did it again!

Telling everyone about my crush on Devon was bad enough. But telling Ross that I lied to him is downright criminal!

"You blabbed again!" I shouted to Mary-Kate in our room. "You told Ross that I went to that photography workshop!"

"I didn't mean to!" Mary-Kate pleaded. "I found out you wanted Ross back, and I wanted to help!"

"How did you find out?" I asked.

Mary-Kate gulped. "Your . . . d-d-diary."

"You read my diary?" I shrieked. "Our second rule as twins is not to read each other's diaries!"

"What's rule number one?" Mary-Kate asked.

"Not to use each other's toothbrushes," I said. "And don't you try to change the subject!"

"Okay, okay," Mary-Kate said. "I picked up your diary by mistake. And I only read one page!"

I folded my arms across my chest.

"You still can't deal with it, can you, Mary-Kate?" I asked. "You still can't accept that I'm winning our bet. So you'll do anything to make my life here the pits!"

"Oh, get real, will you?" Mary-Kate said. "This has nothing to do with our stupid bet!"

"And if you think the bet is off," I said coolly. "You are *wrong*!"

"Fine with me!" Mary-Kate said. "And may the best twin win!"

As I stormed out of our room I knew this wasn't just a bet anymore. . . .

This is *war*!

Chapter 14

Friday

Hi, Diary!

Here's a major news flash: I, Mary-Kate Burke, am now a certified scuba diver!

Early this morning we took the written test and in the afternoon we showed off our scuba skills in the pool.

The written test wasn't too tough (even though I had trouble spelling *buoyancy*). What was *really* tough was sitting just a few seats away from Ashley, knowing we weren't speaking to each other. We didn't even give each other our usual thumbs-up sign before the test!

No one knew the results of the test until after dinner. Jenny announced that everyone passed except for Phoebe. Everyone felt sorry for Phoebe, but we still hugged each other and gave high-fives.

Our gross cousin Jeremy dunked his face in his oatmeal and blew 'scuba' bubbles. Cute.

I saw Ashley at the other end of the table. I was still mad but didn't want this fight to go on forever. So I took a deep breath and walked over to her.

"Congratulations," I told her. "You did it."

Ashley frowned. Then she dropped a bombshell.

"Mary-Kate, when we get back to Chicago I'm going to ask Dad for separate rooms," she said. "You can stay in our room, and I'll move up to the attic."

What? Ashley was taking this too far!

"Don't you remember what happened once before when I moved up to the attic?" I asked her.

"I finally had a neat room for a change?" Ashley said.

"Ashley," I said. "When I moved up to the attic I thought I heard bats!"

"There are no bats in our house, Mary-Kate," Ashley said. "Only RATS!"

I felt my face turn red. Did she mean—me?

"Um, Ashley," Summer said. "You'd better finish your lemon sherbet. Before it gets cold."

Rats!

I spun around and marched back to my side of the table. Not only is Ashley dragging this fight all the way to Chicago, she's still blaming me for something I never did!

And that stinks!

Shore Thing

Dear Diary,

Scuba! Scuba! Scuba!

Today I got my scuba certificate and it felt great. In fact, everybody passed the test except for Phoebe.

"You mean I failed?" Phoebe cried.

"Sorry, Phoebe," Jenny said. "But before you get your scuba certificate you have to go underwater."

Ross passed the test. So did Mary-Kate.

Which means Mary-Kate and I are both winning the bet. In fact, the score is practically tied.

But there's still hope.

This bet isn't just about passing the scuba test. It's also about doing well in every single camp activity.

There's still that canoe race on the swamp tomorrow. And if there are enough spiders and snakes, Mary-Kate might still freak!

Oh, well, Diary, gotta fly.

There's another beach party tonight. And if I'm lucky, Ross will accept my roasted marshmallow peace offering!

See ya!

Chapter 15

Saturday

Dear Diary,

The big canoe race came right after breakfast.

"You'll be split up into teams of two this time," Sid said when we reached the swamp. "All you have to do is follow the red flag markers until you reach the finish point. The first canoe that comes in—wins!"

I didn't ask Ross to team up. Last night at the party he refused to even talk to me. So I chose Elise.

Elise and I threw our backpacks into the canoe. Then we shoved our boat into the swamp and jumped in. Elise took the front. I took the back.

I looked over my shoulder at the others. Mary-Kate was getting into a boat with Phoebe.

The swamp became muckier and narrower as we paddled on. Soon there were no other canoes in sight. Just deer, pelicans, and squawking birds.

"Are you and Mary-Kate still not talking?" Elise asked as she worked her oar.

"Last I checked," I said.

"That's too bad." Elise sighed. "You don't know how lucky you are to have a twin sister."

"A twin that blabs!" I scoffed.

"But Mary-Kate said she didn't tell!" Elise said.

"Then who did?" I asked.

"Beats me," Elise said. "When I went down to breakfast everybody was already talking about it. I think Jeremy started it."

"Then Mary-Kate told Jeremy," I said.

"Are you sure?" Elise asked.

"Mary-Kate and I were the only ones in the dining room when I told her about Devon," I said with a shrug.

Elise looked over her shoulder.

"Dining room?" she said. "That explains it!"

"Huh?" I asked.

"Taco the parrot!" Elise cried. "That blabbermouth with a beak repeats everything he hears!"

I stopped paddling and tried to remember everything Mary-Kate and I said to each other in the dining room.

Then it hit me.

"Elise!" I said. "Mary-Kate said 'Ashley loves Devon' a few times. And Taco was there!"

"Come to think of it," Elise said. "When we asked Jeremy how he knew, he said a little birdie told him. But who knew he meant a *real* bird?"

"Oh, great!" I groaned. But I wasn't mad at the

parrot. I was mad at myself for blaming Mary-Kate. And not listening to her when she told me she was innocent.

Maybe Mary-Kate was right about the diary, too, I thought. Maybe she *did* open it by accident. And maybe she *couldn't* help spilling the beans about the photography workshop.

"What are you going to do now?" Elise asked as we paddled under a canopy of moss.

"What else can I do?" I asked. "As soon as I see Mary-Kate I'm declaring a truce!"

"It's about time!" Elise said. "Now let's win this race!"

I smiled as I pushed my oar into the soupy swamp. I was wrong about Mary-Kate. But it wasn't too late to make things right!

Elise and I didn't win the race, but we came really close. Our canoe came in second and the counselors greeted us at the finish point with cheers and a yummy barbecue.

And the reason I'm writing to you is that Mrs. Clare had to drive back to the house for some hot dog buns. I helped her grab a few bottles of ketchup, then ran up to my room to find you.

I expected to see Mary-Kate at the barbecue

when we got back, but she and Phoebe were a no-show. In fact, practically all of the canoes were in except for theirs.

Oh, well, I thought. Maybe Mary-Kate did freak. She and Phoebe probably just slowed down.

I smiled to myself as I poured ketchup on my burger. The fight may be over.

But the bet was still on!

Dear Diary,

It's a good thing I found you in my backpack, Diary, because you will never believe where I am now.

Give up? I'm stuck in the middle of a swamp!

How did I go from being a camper to a castaway in just a matter of hours? Let me tell you. . . .

After Phoebe and I jumped into our canoes we got a good start. And after already canoeing once, we sort of knew the drill.

"Just keep your eyes on those red flags," I told Phoebe. "And we'll be at the finish point in no time."

"You've become so brave lately, Mary-Kate," Phoebe sighed. "What's your secret?"

"I stopped sweating," I said with a smile. "And started *doing*."

The swamp got thicker and smellier as we kept paddling. I could hear bullfrogs, birds, and lots of crickets.

"I can't believe I failed that scuba test yesterday!" Phoebe said as she pushed the oar through the water.

"You can probably take a scuba course when you get back to San Francisco." I said.

"Who cares about scuba?" Phoebe cried. "It's my article I'm worried about."

"Your article?" I asked.

"I was going to write about my adventures in scuba diving," Phoebe said. "What do I write about now? Beach fashions? Conch chowder? The stuffed alligators in the gift shop?"

"You'll think of something, Phoebe," I said.

As the swamp became narrower the moss on the trees hung lower and lower. I saw a red flag to the right.

"Hang on," I told Phoebe. "This is where we saw those spiders the last time."

"Spiders!" Phoebe stopped paddling. "I can't go under those spiders again. I can't!"

I rested my oar and looked over my shoulder.

Shore Thing

Poor Phoebe was shaking in her 1960s Keds madras sneakers.

"What do you want to do?" I asked Phoebe. "It's not as if we can turn around."

"Then let's take another route!" Phoebe pleaded. She looked around and pointed. "There!"

I looked to see where Phoebe was pointing. A narrow channel ran off in another direction. It was flanked by tall swamp grass.

"Come on, Phoebe," I said. "We wouldn't be following the flags if we went that way."

"Brad said the swamp was circular," Phoebe. "So we'll end up in the same place sooner or later."

"No, Phoebe—"

It was too late. Phoebe was turning the canoe the other way.

"Okay, okay!" I said. "But let's just hope you're right about that circular swamp."

We paddled and paddled for what seemed like forever. The swamp water in the channel became thick as paste. And soon our canoe was stuck in a tangle of mangrove roots!

"I think we're stuck," Phoebe gulped.

"And *lost*!" I declared.

"Lost?" Phoebe gasped. "What do we do?"

"We wait for help, that's what we do!" I said.

A frog jumped into our canoe. It was too much to take, so we climbed out and walked along a giant root leading to a mossy island.

While Phoebe sat hugging her knees I took out my diary. I figured the only way to keep calm was to write.

"You know, Mary-Kate," Phoebe said softly. "Robinson Crusoe had a diary, too."

"Robinson Crusoe?" I wailed. Robinson Crusoe was stranded on an island for decades. By the time they found him, his clothes were tattered and his beard was a mile long. But at least he had coconuts!

"Mary-Kate!" Phoebe said, her dark eyes flashing behind her glasses. "If no one finds us soon we're toast!"

"We should be so lucky," I muttered. "If no one finds us—we're gator chow!"

We sat in silence looking out at the swamp. Diary, the worst that can happen—is now happening to us!

Dear Diary,
I have awful news!

Shore Thing

We waited and waited and waited for Mary-Kate's and Phoebe's canoe to come in, but it never did. Now Sid and the counselors are setting up a search party.

A search party!

Oh, Diary!

Why did I say those horrible things about Mary-Kate? Why didn't I believe her when she said she didn't blab? And what if they never find her again?

What will I ever do without my sister?

Going Places

#18 Two For the Road

Dear Diary,
You'll never guess where I am. Miami!
In a huge hotel on the beach with two
pools and room service and really
cute lifeguards.

Mary-Kate and I have a balcony outside our
room where we can watch the sun set over the ocean
each night. Total bliss.

But I can't relax too much. Practice for the big
triathlon starts tomorrow, and I want to be in super
shape. Especially after what happened today.

Mrs. Clare met with all of us as soon as we got
here to let us know the deal.

"You'll be competing for three days against
fourteen other schools from all over the East
Coast," she explained. "The three sports will be

...ng, beach volleyball, and waterskiing."

Phoebe raised her hand. "Can we pick which sport we want to participate in?" she asked, sounding a little nervous. "I mean, I've never even been waterskiing before."

I tried to imagine Phoebe bouncing over the waves in her vintage 1940s bathing suit. It wasn't easy.

"No, I'm afraid not," Mrs. Clare answered. "One of the rules of the triathlon is that everyone on each team must complete all three events."

A few kids groaned. Phoebe was one of them.

"Don't worry if you're not experienced," Mrs. Clare went on. "The emphasis is on team spirit and cooperation. Remember, the triathlon is going to raise money to save Florida wildlife. For every team that finishes, the sponsors will donate a thousand dollars to the Wildlife Fund."

"Don't *we* get anything for all our hard work?" Jeremy grumbled.

Mrs. Clare grinned. "The team that shows the best sportsmanship will win a special prize," she said. "Now, the first thing you have to do is pick a team captain."

Team captain? I thought. *That would be me*!

Okay, so I'm not all that great at volleyball. But

I'm a whiz on a bicycle. And I learned to water-ski on Lake Michigan near Chicago.

But none of that really matters anyway. What I do best is motivate. Organize. Inspire.

I nudged Mary-Kate. "Nominate me," I whispered.

Mary-Kate seemed startled. She must have been thinking of something else. But just as she began to raise her hand, we heard a familiar voice behind us. Much too familiar.

"Hi guys," Dana Woletsky said. "What's up?"

Oh, no! What was *she* doing here?

Heads whipped around. Summer jumped up and ran to give Dana a big hug. Ross waved at her.

Mrs. Clare beamed. "Dana! We're so glad you could join us. Dana's family has returned early from a cruise in the Bahamas," she explained, "so she'll be with us for the rest of the trip. And just in time to help us choose a team captain."

Summer's hand shot up. "I nominate Dana," she said quickly.

"I second her," Ross said.

That made me so upset, I was hardly paying attention when Mary-Kate nominated me for team captain, too. How could Ross side with Dana after all we've been through together? I know he's still angry with me about Devon. But he knows it was just a misunderstanding. Why can't he just get over it?

Anyway, Diary we're going to vote on team captain tomorrow. I've got to get out there and drum up some support. So that means now I have two goals: Beat Dana for team captain. And get Ross back!

Dear Diary,

Okay. Stay calm. Don't panic. Maybe it's not as bad as it seems.

I'm writing this on hotel stationery. Because my real diary is . . . MISSING!!!

Let me take a deep breath and start at the beginning.

This morning we all piled on the bus for Miami. I tossed my suitcase in the storage space under the bus along with everyone else's and took a seat next to Ashley. Then I started to rummage through my backpack for my diary.

It wasn't there.

I was pretty annoyed. But I figured I probably left it in my suitcase. No big deal.

But the first thing I did when we got to our hotel room was unpack my suitcase and fish through it.

Still no diary.

It was all I could think about during Mrs. Clare's

orientation talk on the triathlon. And now I'm back in my room, going through everything again.

Ashley's over on her bed, writing in her diary. She has this really determined look on her face. Maybe I put my diary in *her* backpack instead. Should I tell Ashley it's missing? Or should I just search her backpack when she isn't looking?

Maybe I shouldn't worry so much. I don't want Ashley to know I'm totally freaked out. And hey, what could I have written that's so bad?

Ha! A lot.

No one can ever find out what I wrote in my diary. If they do, I might as well give up and go back to Chicago. My life at White Oak would be over.

No one would ever talk to me again!

Can Mary-Kate and Ashley Keep a Secret?
Find out in their NEW movie

Mary-Kate Olsen   **Ashley Olsen**

Our Lips Are Sealed

**Filmed in
Sydney, Australia**

DUALSTAR
VIDEO

TM & © 2000 Dualstar Entertainment Group, Inc. Distributed by Warner Home Video.

mary-kateandashley
Magical Mystery Mall™

Available Now

PlayStation

GAME BOY COLOR

GAME BOY COLOR — get a clue!

MAKE YOUR OWN MOVIE MAGIC™
WITH THE
MARY-KATE AND ASHLEY
CELEBRITY PREMIERE FASHION DOLLS

AVAILABLE MARCH 2001!

Go behind the scenes as Mary-Kate gets ready...

...and Ashley sets the scene.

DUALSTAR
ONSUMER PRODUCTS

outta-site!
mary-kateandashley.com

mary-kateandashley

MATTEL

You Are Invited to Join
Mary-Kate and Ashley on a

7-Day
Caribbean Cruise

this Summer, July 1-8, 200

Imagine 7 days and nights at sea on a grand cruise ship with
Mary-Kate and Ashley as you cruise the islands of the eastern Caribbean
aboard Holland America's magnificent ship, the *ms. Maasdam*.

Come visit our website for details at www.sailwiththestars.com or have
an adult call Sail With The Stars at 805-778-1611, M-F • 9:00 am - 5:00 pm PST.

Adventures for a Summer.
Memories for a Lifetime.

outta-site!
mary-kateandashley.com
Register Now

Listen to Us!

Greatest Hits

Ballet Party™

Brother For Sale™

I Am The Cute One™

Sleepover Party™

Birthday Party™

Mary-Kate & Ashley's
CDs and Cassettes
Available Now Wherever
Music is Sold

Lightyear
Entertainment

DUALSTAR
RECORDS

outta site!
mary-kateandashley.com
Register Now

Check out
"Now Read This" on
mary-kateandashley.com
for an exclusive
on-line chapter preview
of our upcoming book!

DUALSTAR
ONLINE